THE BEAR

DETECTIVES

For Sebastien Viveash
– I know your grandma and grandpa!
S.G.

For Izzy
J.B.

ORCHARD BOOKS
338 Euston Road, London NW1 3BH
Orchard Books Australia
Hachette Children's Books
Level 17/207 Kent Street, Sydney NSW 2000

First published by Orchard Books in 2009
First paperback publication in 2010

Text © Sally Grindley 2009
Illustrations © Jo Brown 2009

ISBN 978 1 84616 157 5 (hardback)
ISBN 978 1 84616 165 0 (paperback)

1 3 5 7 9 10 8 6 4 2 (hardback)
1 3 5 7 9 10 8 6 4 2 (paperback)

Printed in China

Orchard Books is a division of Hachette Children's Books,
an Hachette UK company.

www.hachette.co.uk

The Missing Spaghetti

Written by **SALLY GRINDLEY**
Illustrated by **JO BROWN**

ORCHARD BOOKS

Constable Tiggs

Sergeant Bumble

Rupert

Emily

Ollie

Jenny

Mrs Peabody

One morning, Bumble and Tiggs
were drinking tea when the telephone
rang. Bumble answered it.

"Sergeant Bumble at your service.
How may I help you?"

As he listened he raised his
eyebrows higher and higher.
"That's serious," he said, "very
serious, but nothing my constable
and I can't handle."

Bumble put the receiver down.
"What's happened?" asked Tiggs
excitedly.
"Someone has stolen Mrs Peabody's
spaghetti!" exclaimed Bumble.

"Wow!" cried Tiggs. "That is serious!"
"Take your notepad and pencil,
Constable Tiggs," said Bumble.
"We must go and investigate."

They jumped into their car.
"We're on our way!" cried Tiggs.
TOOT TOOT, TOOT TOOT!

Mrs Peabody was waiting
outside her house.

"Thank goodness you're here!" cried
Mrs Peabody. "I put my spaghetti
by the kitchen window, and when
I looked round it had gone!"

12

"Was the window open?" asked Bumble.

"Wide open," said Mrs Peabody.

"So the thief—"

"Or thieves," said Tiggs.

"The thief, or thieves, must have stolen the spaghetti through the window," said Bumble.

"Let's see if there are any
footprints outside," said Tiggs.
"Just what I was going to say,"
said Bumble.

"There are footprints," said Bumble.
"There are definitely footprints."

"I've counted four different sorts
and they're all small," said Tiggs.

"Ah," said Bumble,
"then whatever made
them has small feet."

17

"Look, Sergeant Bumble!"
squealed Tiggs. "There's a trail
of spaghetti!"

"So there is," exclaimed Bumble.
"If we follow it, we might find the
thieves," said Tiggs.
"Just what I was going to say,"
said Bumble.

They began to follow the spaghetti.
It went along the pavement...

...round a lamppost...

...through the supermarket...

...and into the park.

21

"The trail ends here," said Tiggs.
"Thank goodness," puffed Bumble.
"I am quite worn out."

A little way ahead of them they
saw Rupert, Ollie, Emily and
Jenny leaping about and laughing.

"Let's ask those young bears over there if they've seen any more spaghetti," said Tiggs.
"Jolly good idea," said Bumble.
They went over to where the bears were playing hopscotch.

"I'm sorry to disturb your game, young bears," said Bumble, "but we're looking for some missing spaghetti. Have you seen any?"

The bears stopped playing and
shuffled their feet.

"I've found it, Sergeant Bumble!"
cried Tiggs.
"Where?" asked Bumble.
"Look at the hopscotch
squares," said Tiggs.
"Well I never!"
cried Bumble.

"We only borrowed it," said
Rupert.
"We were going to give it back,"
said Emily.

"That's all very well," said Bumble sternly, "but Mrs Peabody is very upset. You will have to say sorry to her, and I shall expect you to help her with the gardening for a week."

"Yes, Sir, Sergeant Bumble, Sir,"
said the bears, and they ran off
to find Mrs Peabody.
"That's another mystery solved,
then," said Bumble. "Well done,
Constable Tiggs."

"Thank you,
Sergeant Bumble,"
smiled Tiggs.
"Time for a
nice cup of tea!"
said Bumble.

SALLY GRINDLEY & JO BROWN

Bucket Rescue	978 1 84616 160 5
Who Shouted Boo?	978 1 84616 159 9
The Ghost Train	978 1 84616 161 2
Treasure Hunt	978 1 84616 158 2
The Mysterious Earth	978 1 84616 163 6
The Strange Pawprint	978 1 84616 164 3
The Missing Spaghetti	978 1 84616 165 0
A Very Important Day	978 1 84616 162 9

All priced at £4.99

Orchard Colour Crunchies are available from all good bookshops,
or can be ordered direct from the publisher:
Orchard Books, PO BOX 29, Douglas IM99 1BQ
Credit card orders please telephone 01624 836000
or fax 01624 837033 or visit our website: www.orchardbooks.co.uk
or e-mail: bookshop@enterprise.net for details.

To order please quote title, author and ISBN
and your full name and address.
Cheques and postal orders should be made payable to 'Bookpost plc.'
Postage and packing is FREE within the UK
(overseas customers should add £2.00 per book).

Prices and availability are subject to change.